This work seems to have made little impression, either in England or in France, even though it has the remarkable distinction of being illustrated solely by collages drawn from the catalogue of a large department store in London (Whiteley's), and therefore of being— as much by the images as by the text that they comment on—one of the first manifestations of that spirit we call "modern."

Raymond Queneau
Bâtons, chiffres et lettres (1950)

What a Life!

by E.V.L & G.M.

Absurdist Texts & Documents
No. 34

What a Life!
by E. V. Lucas & George Morrow

Black Scat Books
Absurdist Texts & Documents (No. 34)

Copyright © 2018 by Black Scat Books

ISBN-13: 978-1-7323506-9-4

This is a reprint of the original British edition published by Methuen & Co. Ltd., in 1911.

This Black Scat trade paperback edition was created from high resolution digital files prepared with love by Stewart C. Russell in Kirkintilloch, Scotland.

Author's portraits courtesy of Wikipedia

The Absurdist Texts & Documents series colophon on the title page is a trademark of Black Scat Books.

Black Scat Books
Publishers of Sublime Art & Literature
BlackScatBooks.net

Publisher's Note

On August 17 1911—seven years before Max
Ernst took up scissors and paste to create his
early Dada art—**WHAT IS LIFE!** was published
in London by Methuen & Co. The authors, Edward Verrall Lucas (a travel writer) and George
Morrow (an illustrator and regular contributor
to *Punch*), produced their satirical autobiog-
raphy using illustrations cut from the pages of
Whiteley's General Catalogue. This inspired act of
artistic vandalism was a precursor to many works
of avant-garde art and satire. Out of print for
years in the United States, Black Scat is pleased
to bring this "deeply-moving human drama" back
to life.

N. C.
Guerneville, California
May, 2018

Preface

AS adventures are to the adventurous, so
is romance to the romantic.   One man
searching the pages of Whiteley's General
Catalogue will find only facts and prices;
another will find what we think we have
found—a deeply-moving human drama.

E. V. L.
G. M.

CONTENTS

Chapter I

CHILDHOOD

I was born very near the end of the year.

The grange where I was born was situated in a secluded corner of the Chiltern Hills. Rumour had it that Queen Elizabeth had slept there.

My father was the soul of hospitality,

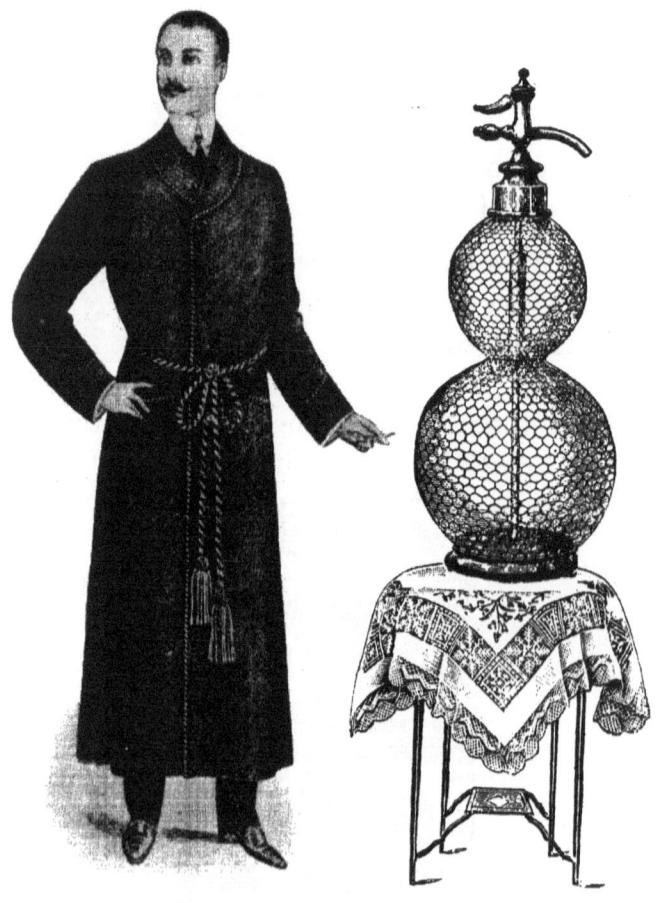

and kept cigars to suit all tastes.

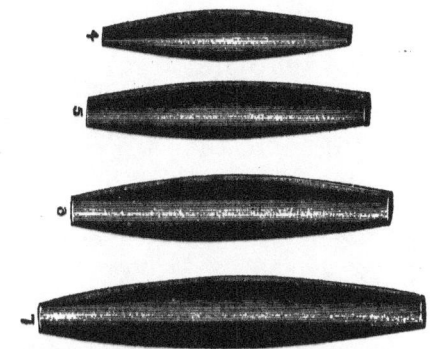

Never a very strong man,

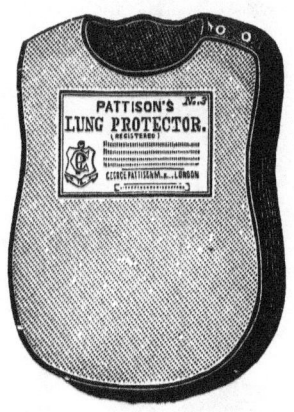

he was perforce a great traveller, and my sweet mother loved to follow his wanderings on the quaint old globe in the library.

Their's was an ideal union. They were sweethearts since the time my mother wore short frocks.

Our house had superb grounds, and the garden was a scene of savage grandeur.

Two swans — one English and one Australian—were always on the lake.

Our head keeper—good fellow!—saw to it that the birds were plentiful.

My father was not only a dead shot,

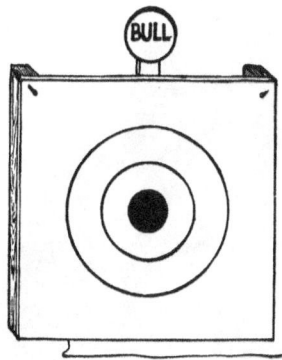

but, as a huntsman, frequently returned home after a long day with the harriers, tired but triumphant, with the brush.

My earliest recollection is of lying in the cradle and wondering if lying was my destiny.

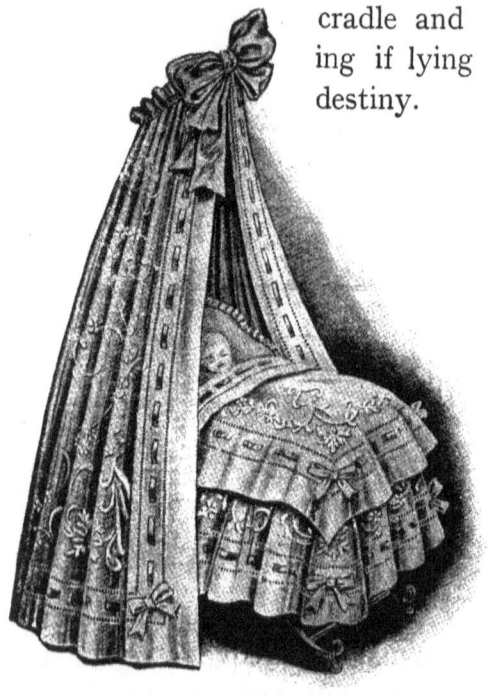

Of all my nurses,
Gregson was my
favourite.

She was the daughter of a poor broken-down clarionet player, but was really a lady in spite of her garb of servitude.

Everyone was kind to me. Our Dutch gardener adored me,

and I was a prime favourite with our old housekeeper.

But my happiest hours were spent with the little daughter of our neighbour Sir Easton West. She was a pretty child, and, boy-like, I did my best to attract her attention.

Her parents lived in a Tudor manor that was reported to be haunted.

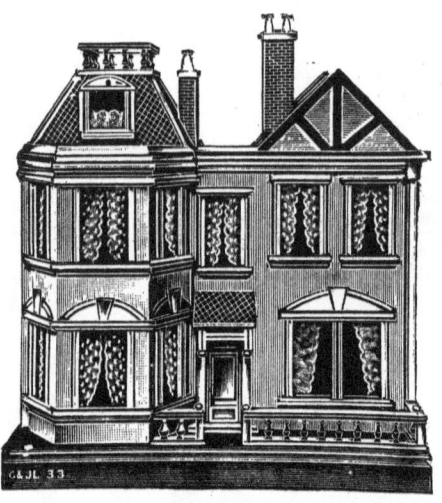

According to the legend whispered by the retainers and villagers, no sooner did the clock strike twelve

than a headless apparition was seen **to** move slowly across the moonlit hall.

Poor Belinda, her fits were frequent.

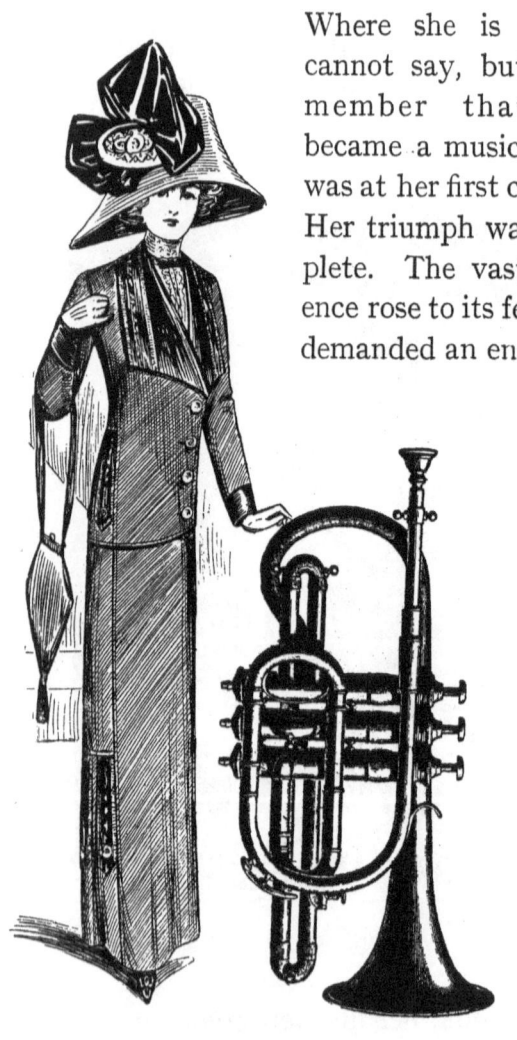

Where she is now I
cannot say, but I re-
member that she
became a musician. I
was at her first concert.
Her triumph was com-
plete. The vast audi-
ence rose to its feet and
demanded an encore.

I pass over other ordinary occurrences incidental to childhood, such as being kidnapped by gipsies,

and my first visit to the dentist,

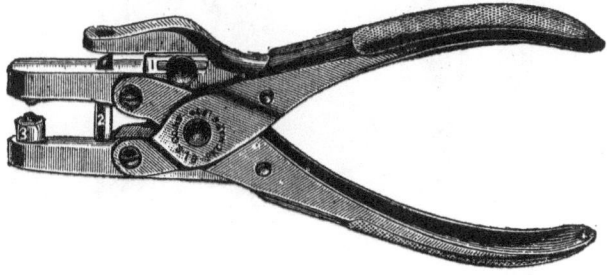

and come to my life at the preparatory school, to which I went to discover whether

I was to serve my country in the Navy or
the Army.

CHAPTER II

SCHOOL DAYS

SCHOOL DAYS! Was there ever a happier time? I was sent to Dr. Bodey's in West Kensington.

The name was on the door—"Dryburgh." You could not mistake it.

Although a martyr to kidney trouble for

years, Dr. Bodey was a powerful man and an adept at all outdoor sports.

He had married a Swiss, a lady as active as himself,

and together they held the championship at Spiro-pole.

A lenient and generous teacher, the Doctor took us often to the Crystal Palace

or to the Zoo.

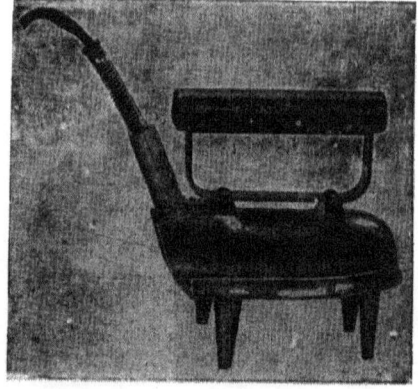

Our favourite game was leapfrog.

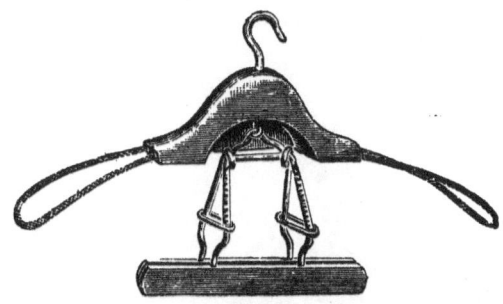

I was at this time a handsome boy of fourteen.

Among my school fellows were some delight-
ful lads,

chiefly the sons of the nobility and clergy.

My closest friend was Eustace Bleek-Wether with whom I often spent the vacations;

and my *bête noire* was the Hon. Harold Crumpton, who made my life at school a perfect hell for the first three months.

His father was a learned and interesting man, with, alas, one sad and only too common failing.

They lived in a beautiful home nestling in the Surrey hills.

We both adored
the matron.

In spite of this rivalry we were friends, and remained so after leaving Dr. Bodey's and passing through the 'Varsity.

Eustace was brilliant in every way. A wonderful fisherman ;

and a crack shot, rarely bringing down his
birds singly.

Once, however, (I remember) he missed his quarry. Time after time he fired, but the bird was still there.

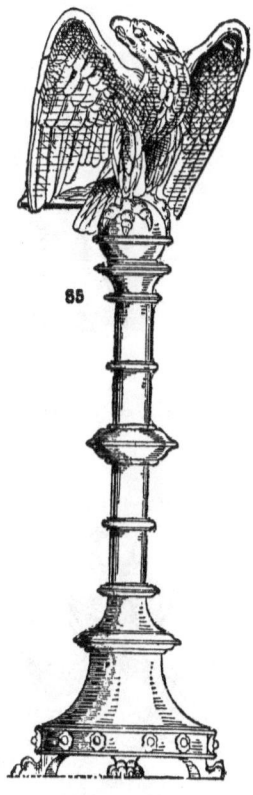

Poor Eustace! a fatal fascination for the Pole gripped him,

and he now lies in a silent grave beneath the Arctic star.

To return to my own story, I left school when I was eighteen and went to Oxford College,

and
at the
age of
t w e n t y -
two I became
a man about
town with a latch-key of my own.

CHAPTER III

LONDON IN THE OLD DAYS

KNOCKING about town as I then did, I naturally got to know many people, especially as I was still unmarried.

For example, Lady Mayfair, the present Queen of Society, I remember as a little toddling child who climbed on my knees.

I knew Monty Wotherspoon, the amateur pyramid champion, intimately.

Monty was one of the old dare-devil crowd. I remember the sensation he caused when, for a wager, he drove a hansom from the Guards' Club to Hurlingham without reins.

Poor fellow, his end was very tragic. He was poisoned by his wife. She had rinsed the glass and removed, as she thought, all traces of the poison; but the Law was too much for her.

The autopsy revealed unmistakable signs of the deadly drug.

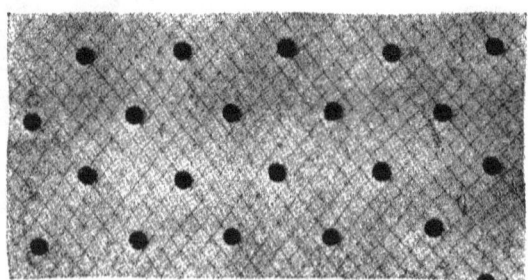

Then there was the Earl of Crewett, who was never seen out of riding breeches: a veritable centaur.

It was Lord Crewett who won the Derby with "Salad Days."

The eccentric Sir William Goosepelt was a friend of mine. Among his other odd ways he often indulged in the luxury of a treacle bath.

Sir William's ears were so large that he required a chin-strap to keep his hat on. From this circumstance he earned an unenviable reputation for impoliteness towards ladies.

His wife, dear Lady Goosepelt, was a chronic invalid, and lived at Bournemouth in a charming *villegiatura*.

Sir William's beautiful mansion was burnt to the ground. It was, I remember, on Sunday, the 23rd.

The alarm was given, but no horses could be procured, so the brigade was at a standstill.

Another man about town at that time was Sir Henry Punt. He and his wife (a beautiful woman) were probably the most inveterate gamblers living.

Lady Punt was one of the few women of fashion who had received the King's Bounty, and I often watched her charming brood bathing in the marble basin in their grounds, which adjoined mine.

Sir Henry (who died only last year) had a weakness for growing mushrooms for harvest festivals.

The Duke of Pudsey, in spite of his great wealth, was of a penurious nature. He was also something of a kleptomaniac, and after his death an extraordinary collection of umbrellas which he had removed from the club stand was discovered.

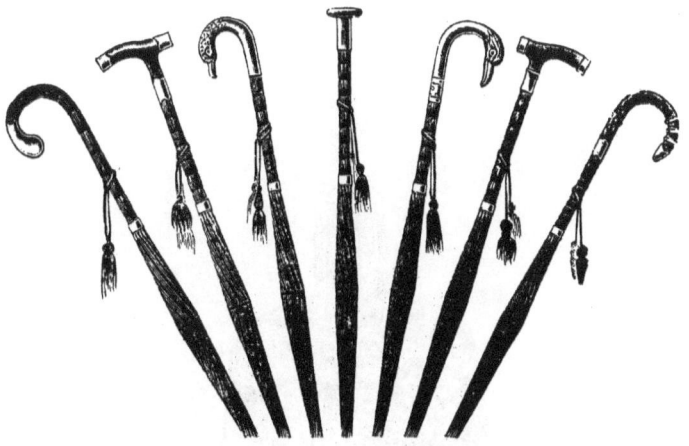

On one occasion he was actually found concealing the watch of one of his guests,

None the less (such is human tolerance of
the great), when the Duke came to die a
magnificent memorial was erected to him.

His son's wife, Lady Clipstone, was one of the most determined autograph hunters I ever met.

The Duke's only daughter, who became Lady Grapholine Meadows, was never seen without her coronet, which was a masterpiece of the jeweller's art.

His other son, Lord Bertie, married the fashionable sister of Lord George Sangazure.

It was about this time that I made the acquaintance of William Browne, of London,

whose peculiarity it was to be always out. It is con-
jectured that during a period of many years he was never at home.

Sir William Broadfoot, the well-known R.A., was a frequent visitor. He would often go out sketching, but was so absent-minded that he forgot his paints.

Then there was Lord Highlow, who con-
structed a dirigible of his own invention, in
which he made fre-
quent ascents from
Brooklands, accom-
panied by his two
beautiful daughters.

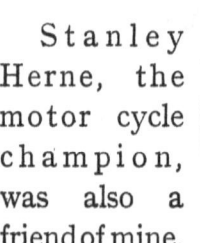

Stanley
Herne, the
motor cycle
champion,
was also a
friend of mine.
Alas ! he rides no more, not since that
terrible collision with a motor bus. There

lay Stanley, a ruin of what he was, while the heavy vehicle, crowded with happy passengers, all unconscious of what had happened, rolled on.

I knew slightly Sir Algernon Slack, the millionaire, whose peculiarity it was never to carry an umbrella.

One of this strange man's peculiarities was that he could not endure the presence of a cat.

His end, it is thought, was quickened by varicose veins in the right hand.

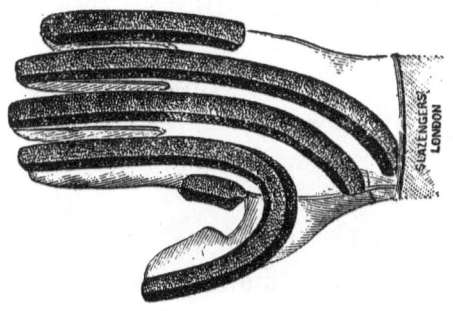

He died in 1901, and was buried next his wife.

CHAPTER IV

THE STOLEN DIAMONDS

ONE of the most interesting occurrences of my crowded life was my participation in the famous Closure Castle jewel robbery.

I was staying with Lord Bunderbourne. His old Jacobean mansion embowered in trees was an ideal spot for a daring burglary.

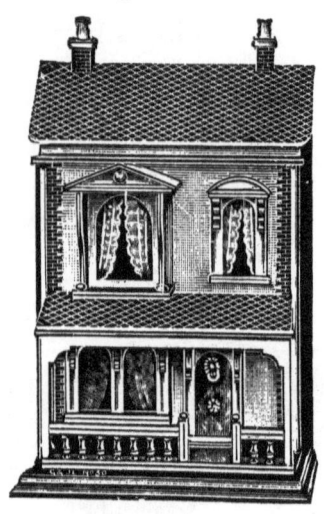

It was, I remember, mid-winter. The fountain was frozen.

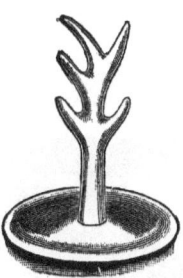

We had just finished dinner

when the local constable burst in to say that a convict had escaped from the neighbouring prison.

It was too true.   The safe was empty.

Our cigars were forgotten in the excitement
of the moment.

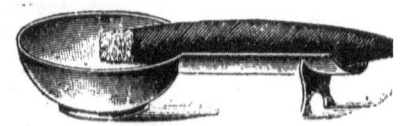

A detective was telephoned for, and came at once.

He first made a plan of the house,

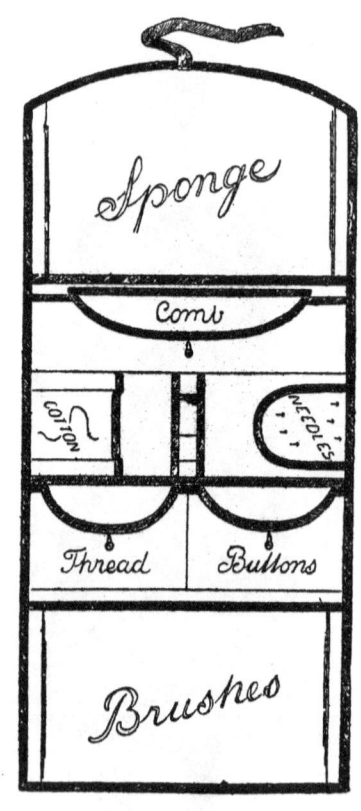

and hurried next to the kitchen garden, where he stood aghast at his discovery.

Then on to the out-houses, where it was noticed that one of the doors was partly open.

Ponto, the watch dog, seemed dazed.   He had been drugged, the detective said.

He also pointed out that the horse's neck was strangely swollen.

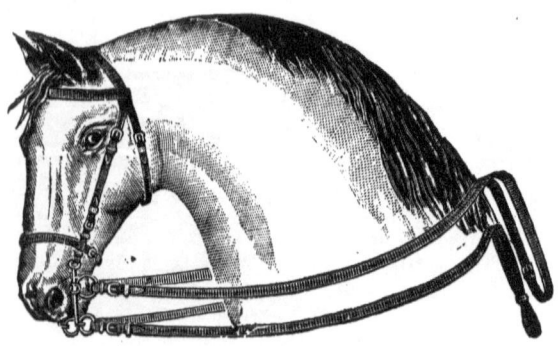

The detective next interrogated the whole house party, although some were in *déshabille*.

Suspicion fell first on the chief footman,
whose embarrass-
ment was greatly
in his disfavour.

Passing to the man's room the detective saw at a glance that the bed had not been slept on.

Meanwhile, being alone in the drawing room, I had an instinctive feeling that someone was hiding behind the screen,

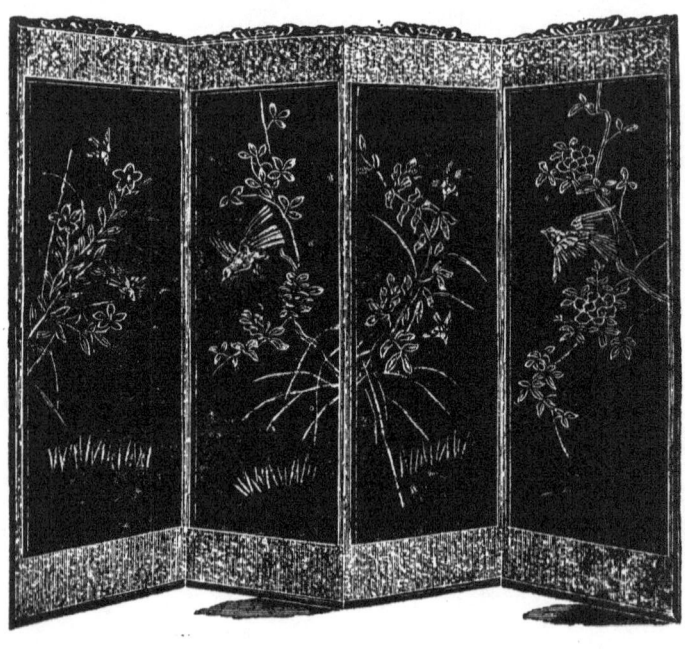

and I was certain that I heard the sound of the sharpening of a knife.

Having no other weapon handy, I produced my toothpick.

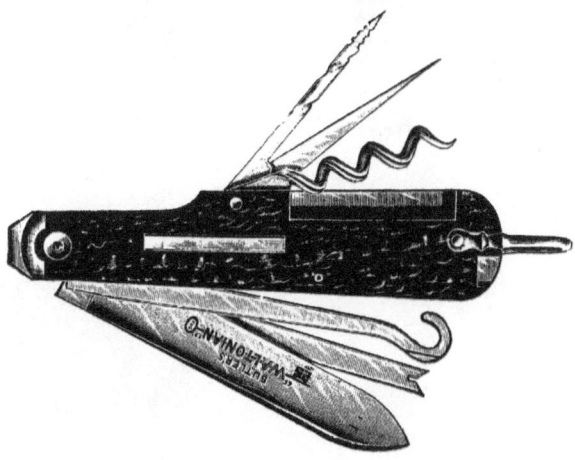

But at this moment the detective returned, in a disguise calculated to baffle the keenest observer.

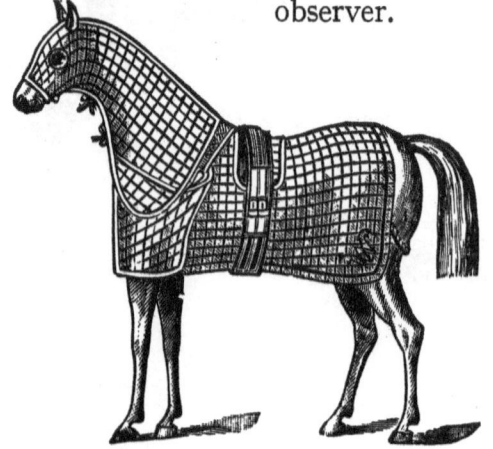

The contents of the mysterious bag having been analysed,

he showed us that the ring was movable,

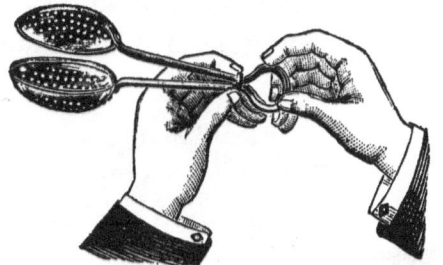

and drew our attention to the fact that there were signs of a struggle.

He then showed us the print of a blood-stained hand on the wall, and producing his pocket book, convinced us that in spite of certain superficial differences, they were one and the same man.

We were immensely impressed, and in a few moments the burglar was fairly trapped.

The detective then resumed his natural appearance,

and was presented by Lord Bunderbourne with a heavy cheque.

While waiting for the prison van

he told us some good stories of his career. It was he, it seems, who was the real hero of the Charlotte Street anarchist plot, which he discovered by overhearing a conversation between two of the miscreants in a Soho restaurant.

He gave us also some curious information about the ingenious methods of famous c r i m i n a l s. There was, for example, the notorious one-eyed Jimmy Snaffles, who used a house-breaking implement of his own construction, which he  would try on the trees outside before breaking into the house.

And there were that very respectable couple, Tom Bilks and his wife, who entered houses with scaling ladders at night, and kept a blameless registry office in Balham through the day.

Chapter V

THE TENDER PASSION

It is idle to deny that I was a hand-some man.

Some-thing also of a dandy, my appeal to women must have been terrific.

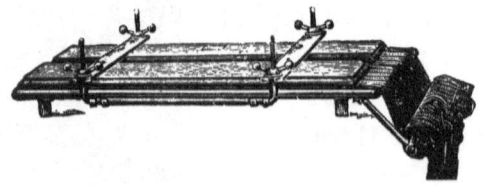

They were also attracted by my Norman descent, for it was common knowledge that one of my ancestors, Sir Ikimo de Medici, had come over with the Conqueror.

Always susceptible, I quickly fell in love. My first *innamorata* was the daughter of a lion tamer, and herself, although a Suffragette, in that romantic profession.

Her father disapproved of the intimacy, and
we had to correspond clandestinely.   She
would write and seal her letter, and then
place it inside a football, and leave it for me
in the place agreed upon.

My second love was the lady golf
champion of Golder's Green.

Dear Honoria — she inherited from her uncle, Sir Felix Chalk-stones, one of the neatest ankles in the Home Counties.

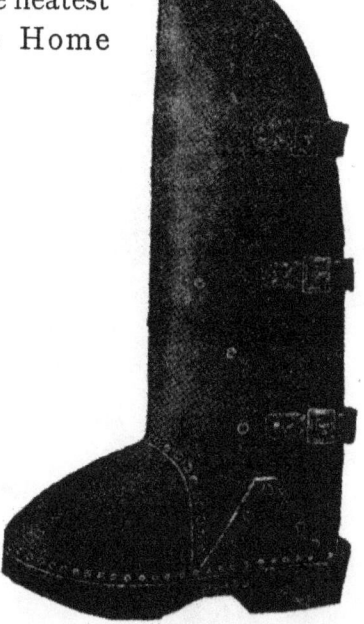

Unfortunately she was a deaf mute, and when we met our sweet nothings had to be conveyed by the clumsy method of sign language.

My third was Lily,
who never wrote, but
communicated with me
on the telephone.

—Dear, brave Lily, who in the dark days struggled so hard to support her mother and poor ailing Susan.

But at last I met my fate—Lady Brenda
Birdseye. I had motored over to her
father's seat—Cavendish Court. I wandered
through the house; it was empty. Lunch
was not yet cleared away.

The tennis court was deserted ;

but in a hammock in the shrubbery I chanced upon her—asleep. It seemed a pity to disturb her dreams. I gazed, and was fascinated.

Fond fool—I thought that Lady Brenda smiled upon me.　She seemed to like me to pay for her lunch.　We were often to be seen together at Ranelagh.

But I was living in a fool's paradise—she loved another. The news came to me as I was eating my breakfast.

Could it be true? But to whom was she engaged? To Lord Kempton, that cur.

What was I to do? To hail and leap into a taxi was the work of a moment.

The maid said she was not at home. I said I *must* see her. She saw me. I heard afterwards how she had braced herself for the effort.

I vowed to be revenged on my rival, even if I had to follow him to the bottom of the sea.

She gave me no hope and I left her in despair. For days I lived on nothing but a few sandwiches.

Then I grew more philosophic and tried other means to forget her,

but in vain. It was no good, I took to my bed; and for some months my life was despaired of.

On recovering sufficiently, I determined to seek peace of mind in travel.

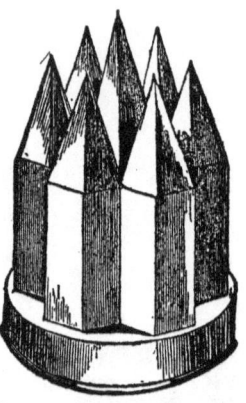

CHAPTER VI

TRAVEL AND ADVENTURE

IN the mad effort to forget Lady Brenda
I globe-trotted furiously.

One day found me among the quaint
walled towns of Normandy.

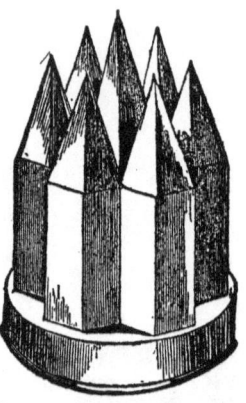

The next I was in Germany.

Feeling that excitement was necessary to me, I joined the motor race to Monte Carlo,

and was to be seen every night in the Casino;

where I lost heavily.

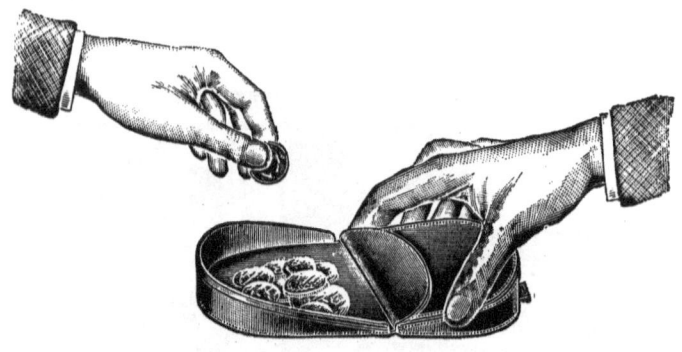

I passed on to Venice,

and from there to Naples.

But in vain—I could not forget Lady
Brenda, and sleep was out of the question.

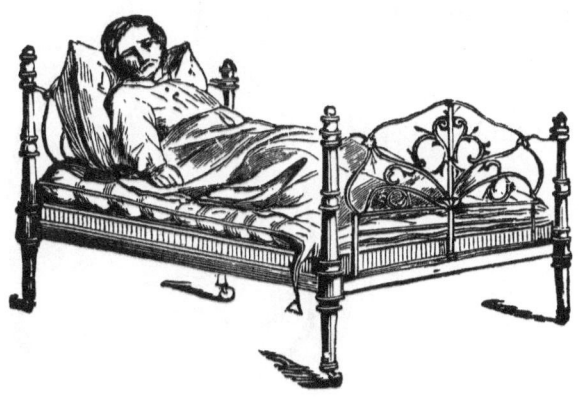

I also suffered from loss of **memory**, and frequently **forgot** my shirt and waistcoat.

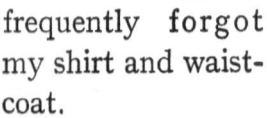

In my despair I took for a brief, mad period to drink, but was careful that no one should suspect the proximity of the bottle.

From Naples I passed on to India, that land

of mystery and Eastern splendour.

It was my first experience of the tropics. The heat was intense.

JANUARY

Wednesday

1

At night I lay with my tent open;

by day the jungle throbbed beneath the intolerable sun.

But by taking precautions I retained my
health.

I had also my faithful and admirable syce,
who, like everyone with whom I have
ever come in contact (except, alas! Lady
Brenda), adored
me.

Then came the Paticaka Guerilla War. I enlisted against the insurgent Gherkins.

I slept soundly the night before the battle.

Although shot many times I fought on, but I became unconscious from loss of blood, not, however, until the day was won. That night eleven bullets, which I still preserve, were extracted from my body.

The Maharajah showed his appreciation
of my services,

and, furthermore, put me to the blush by
offering me his favourite wife.

It was on leaving Paticaka that I had the narrowest escape from death that I have yet experienced.   I took my seat in the Calcutta train

and settled myself to repose, when, with a fearful crash, the carriage was overturned. We had disregarded the signal.

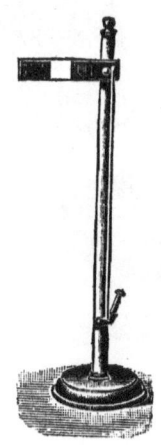

The scene was appalling; human remains strewed the ground.

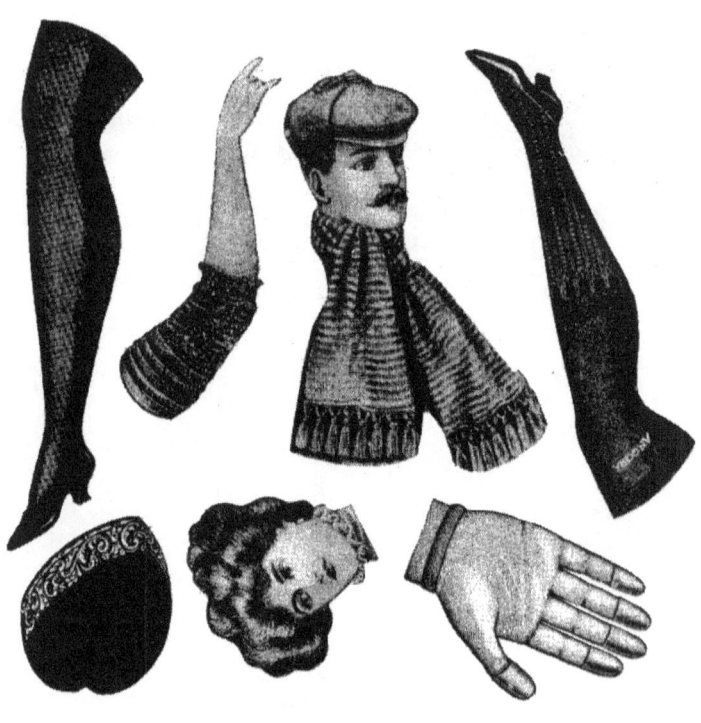

Fortunately I escaped unhurt, although somewhat badly shaken.

Before returning to England I visited Japan,

where I made many friends among the quaint little people. I saw a sight I shall never forget—the sun rising over Fusiyama.

Later in the day I saw it set—an equally memorable spectacle.

AFTER USE

From Japan I sailed to Africa, and among the many photographs I took is a view of a kraal on the banks of the Oomba river, Nygskmbasi, B.C.A.

CHAPTER VII

HOME LIFE

I T was on the liner coming back,

just off (I remember) the Eddystone light-
house,

that I met my dear wife.

She was the daughter of a retired Government official, now

enjoying a leisurely and happy old age.

We had long been catching each other's eyes. The time was ripe. When I at last proposed, she gave me both hands impulsively.

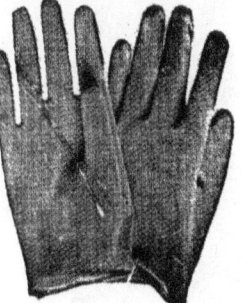

Ours was a romantic engagement,

but we decided to cut it very short, and were married directly the village church could be made ready.

We had some very novel wedding presents.

My best man was Lord Wagglecleek.

Almost my oldest friend, I
had first met him in the bath.

It was a pretty service, and the villagers,
whose hearts are wholly ours,

gave us a cordial send-off.

We were idyllically happy at Frisby Towers, in spite of its outward air of gloom.

We both had rural tastes. My wife was very fond of whipping the stream,

and I was, of
course, an ardent
golfer.

One day we took
the motor;

on the next I ordered out the roan.

When it rained we knew what to do.

We were so simple that
we often did not dress for
dinner.

In the evening after a small but *recherché*
meal, for the *cuisine* at Frisby Towers left
nothing to be desired,

we had music.   Melba's divine notes floated
into the liquid air,

or I would perform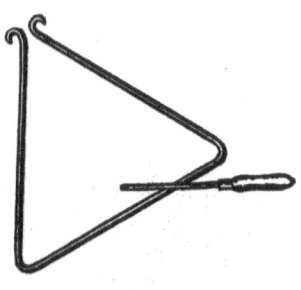
a solo on my favour-
ite instrument,
which I flatter my-
self I play with a
certain amount of
delicacy and feeling ;

my wife occasionally ac-
companying me on the
harp.

We entertained freely.
Like my father I am a most
hospitable man.

No sooner is a guest
inside my doors, than I
pass the refreshments.

In other
ways also I
kept them
a m u s e d
and happy.

By day we often made up parties of six for
the fishing.

I had my hobbies too.

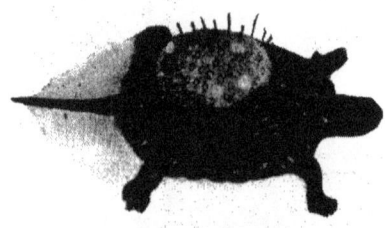

In 1904 I succeeded, after many failures, in obtaining a cross between a tortoise and a porcupine, and the training of the hybrid gives me infinite pleasure.

I was also the foremost conchologist of the country, and the arranging of my collection of 14,000 varieties of winkles, now in the Natural History Museum, occupied many otherwise tedious evenings.

Life also had its
exciting incidents.
Now and then I
would add to my
unique collection
of Sèvres;

or a new hat would
come from London
for my wife.

Sometimes a guest revoked;

while an occasional *fracas* with the plumber also enlivened the routine, as when on one memorable occasion I drew his attention to the inadequacy of the bath.

Now and then my wife and I may even have had a tiff, during which we were not on speaking terms ; but it soon blew over.

On Sunday we naturally went to church, to which, in my capacity of Squire, I presented a new organ,

and where I frequently had the pleasure of hearing the choir render my favourite hymns.

CHAPTER VIII

APOTHEOSIS.

SUCH was my life for a considerable
period—, rendered really notable only
by the arrival of a son and heir—

until 1911, my *annus mirabilis*. But then
everything was changed, for the Prime
Minister graciously invited me to become

one of his new peers, which I was pleased
to agree to; and I therefore take my leave
of my patient and too indulgent readers as
Baron Dropmore, of Corfe.

About the Authors

Edward Verrall Lucas, (1868 – 1938). Born outside London in Eltham, Kent, Lucas was a writer and humorist who joined the staff of *Punch* in 1904 as an assistant editor and remained there his entire career. In addition to humorous pieces, he wrote poems, novels, plays, and travel books. In 1924, he was appointed chairman of the British publishing house Methuen and Co.—the original publishers of *What a Life!* (1911).

George Morrow, (1869 – 1955). Born in Belfast, Morrow was a book illustrator and cartoonist. His comic parodies of Royal Academy pictures ("Royal Academy Depressions") became a popular series. He contributed to many periodicals, including the *Bystander*, *Strand Magazine*, and *Tatler*. Several collections of his cartoons were published, including *Alphabet of the War* (1915); *George Morrow: His Book* (1920); *More Morrow* (1921).

Self-portrait (1920)

BLACK SCAT BOOKS in print